FOR MY EDITOR,
ANAMIKA BHATNAGAR

CHAPTERS

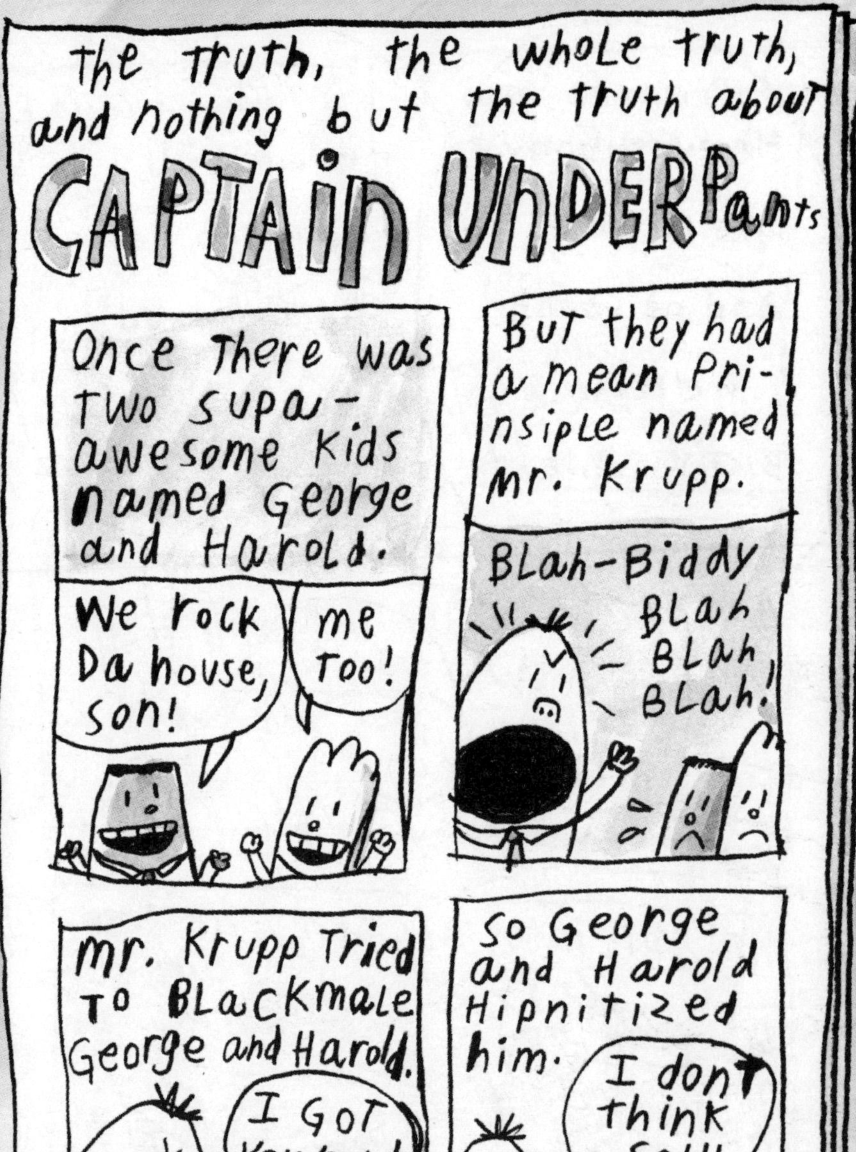
The truth, the whole truth, and nothing but the truth about
CAPTAIN UNDERPants
Once There was Two supa-awesome Kids named George and Harold.
We rock Da house, son!
me Too!
But they had a mean Pri-nsiple named mr. Krupp.
Blah-Biddy Blah Blah Blah!
mr. Krupp Tried To Blackmale George and Harold.
I Got You now!
Video Evide-nse
So George and Harold Hipnitized him.
I dont think so!!!

They made him think He was captain underpants!

it was funny at First...

But then He took things a little too far!

Tra-La-Laaaaa!

Hey come Back!

He got into all sorts of ~~TROUBLE~~ TROUBeL.

Then one day he drank some alien super power juice...

...and he got REAL Super powers.

Wich got him into even more TrouBel.

Now, whenever Mr. Krupp Hears somebody Snap thier Fingers...

SNAP

...He Turns into Captain Underpants.

Tra-La Laaaa!

the robo PLunger Beated uP the Turbo Toilet 2000

and FLew him to uranus.

welcome to uranus

THere they have stayed for many months.

This other time, wedgie woman made 2 robots.

One of them Kicked a kickball into outer space.

could these two events Be ~~that~~ connected ?

Our heros are about to find out!

Because at this very mo- mint...

they are treveling Backwerds in time to discover the terrible truth!

OH NO!

Here we Go again!

© Tree House comix

CHAPTER 1

GEORGE AND HAROLD

This is George Beard and Harold Hutchins.
George is the kid on the left with the tie
and the flat-top. Harold is the one on the
right with the T-shirt and the bad haircut.
Remember that now.

If you're confused by what's going on here, don't worry. They're confused, too. You see, George, Harold and Captain Underpants had just undergone an epic adventure that started out in the dinosaur age and ended at their school — forty years in the future. Now, thanks to Melvin Sneedly (the tattletale genius) and his glow-in-the-dark, time-travelling Robo-Squid suit, they were all hurtling backwards in time. Back a long, long, long time ago to that dull, old-fashioned age known as the present.

Oh, I almost forgot. Travelling with them were three purple-and-orange-speckled eggs, laid by their pet pterodactyl, Crackers, who, along with their other pet – Sulu the Bionic Hamster – had just saved the planet *and* created all life as we know it, simultaneously.

See? That wasn't confusing at all, was it?

Melvin's glow-in-the-dark, time-travelling Robo-Squid suit whizzed through time in a dazzling array of electrified eye candy as forty years sped by in reverse.

Then everything stopped suddenly.
George and Harold looked around.

"Hey," said Harold. "We're still here at
school!"

"Correct," said Melvin. "Only it's now
forty years and one day earlier."

"Hey, look," said George, pointing at the school. "There's Tippy and his Robo-Pants."

"Not again," Harold moaned.

"Relax," said Melvin, as a flash of green light shot out of the library window. "You're looking at something that happened yesterday, remember?"

"Oh, yeah," said Harold. "We were up there in the library. We just disappeared in the Purple Potty!"

"Right," said George. "And Tippy is just about to come after us. He should be leaving any second now."

Suddenly, a crackling blue light shot out
of the Robo-Pants, and before you could say
"convoluted plotline", it disappeared into the
noontime haze.

"OK," said Melvin. "Here you are. Home
again, home again, jiggity jig! Take your
precious eggs and go about your business!"

"Wait a second," said George. "Aren't the
cops still after us?"

"Yeah," said Harold. "Don't they still think
we stole that money from the bank?"

18

"Not any more," said Melvin proudly, patting himself on the back with one of his mechanical tentacles. "Luckily, I had this glow-in-the-dark, time-travelling Robo-Squid suit in my garage. I used it to go back in time and hack into the bank's computer."

"What for?" asked Harold.

"No big deal," said Melvin. "I altered their surveillance images a little bit. Just don't grow a moustache or a beard anytime soon, and you guys'll be fine."

"Wow," said Harold. "Melvin
Sneedly rescued us. I can't believe it!"

"Yeah, I don't get it, Melvin," said George
suspiciously. "You've always hated us. How
come you're being so nice to us all of a
sudden?"

"Oh, I have my reasons," said Melvin. "I
have my reasons."

And Melvin did indeed have reasons. One
whole year's worth of reasons. But before
I can tell you that story, I have to tell you
this story. . .

CHAPTER 2

DON'T YOU HATE IT WHEN A KICKBALL HITS URANUS?

Somewhere in the deepest, darkest reaches of our solar system, a red, rubber kickball was zooming through space. None of Earth's top scientists could explain where it had come from, or why it was racing towards Uranus, but it had been on its present course for the past five and a half books, and nothing could stop it.

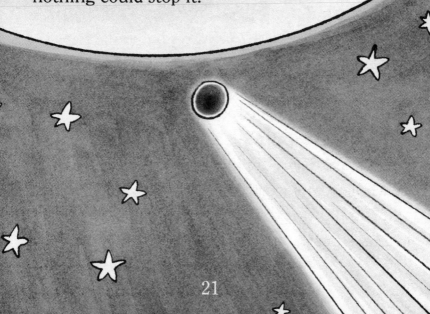

The kickball sped closer and closer to a small cluster of porcelain monstrosities that lay together in a heap on the surface of the icy, ridiculously named planet. Behind them, guarding them all with a keen, observant eye, was a robotic sentinel known as the Incredible Robo-Plunger. Faster and faster the kickball whizzed towards them, until finally. . .

The force of the red, rubber ball
knocked the head right off of the
Incredible Robo-Plunger. The decapitated
defender jutted forward slightly, as
Photo-Atomic Trans-Somgobulating
Yectofantriplutoniczanziptomistic juice
drizzled out from its mangled neck hole
and oozed slowly downward into the
gaping mouth of the Turbo Toilet 2000.

23

This was unfortunate, because as any robotics engineer will tell you, it's very important to keep Photo-Atomic Trans-Somgobulating Yectofantriplutoniczanziptomistic juice as far away from evil robots as possible.

You certainly don't want to get even a drop of it in their mouths, for it will only make them come to life and give them an unquenchable appetite for destruction. Which, sadly, is exactly what happened that bleak night on the terribly gassy surface of Uranus.

The Turbo Toilet 2000's bulbous, bloodshot eyes smacked open and wobbled around wildly. His massive left arm creaked up and rubbed the painful, throbbing side of his porcelain lid.

"Where the heck am I?" he said, looking around at his fallen allies. Clumsily, he squeaked to his feet, dusted himself off and beheld the headless mess that once was the Incredible Robo-Plunger. Then it all came back to him. The battle. The defeat. The humiliation.

It wasn't long before the Turbo Toilet 2000 had pieced together every single event that had brought him and his army of Talking Toilets to this frozen, frustrating fate.

"I must retaliate," he said, clenching his razor-sharp porcelain teeth together tightly. "I must avenge my fallen allies!"

Luckily for him, he was a robot, which meant that he knew a thing or two about mechanical engineering. It didn't take long for him to disassemble the Robo-Plunger, rearrange the pieces and create a flying rocket scooter from the recycled parts of his arch-enemy.

The only thing left to do was to travel the long journey from Uranus to Earth. It was a voyage that would take him nearly three whole pages to complete. And when he arrived, he would wage a war against the good people of Earth. A war that would threaten the very foundation of our planet. But before I can tell you that story, I have to tell you *this* story. . .

CHAPTER 3

MELVIN'S MOMENT OF MIRTH

Remember back in chapter 1 where we found out that Melvin had a whole year's worth of reasons why he needed to bring George and Harold and Captain Underpants back to the present? Well, in case you're wondering what happened during that year, here's what happened during that year:

Immediately after our heroes disappeared on their prehistoric journey, the cops started looking for George, Harold and Mr Krupp. Wanted posters appeared in post offices across America. But, since George and Harold and Mr Krupp had travelled back in time to the Cretaceous period, they were nowhere to be found.

Everyone assumed that George, Harold and Mr Krupp had robbed a bank and were hiding out in Canada or Mexico somewhere, and it wasn't too long before the cops gave up and stopped looking for them.

This was sad news for most of the residents of Piqua, Ohio, but not for Melvin Sneedly. Melvin was finally happy for the first time in years. No George and no Harold meant no pranks, no comics, and, best of all, no interruptions. Melvin could finally go about conducting his scientific experiments, creating wild new inventions and indulging his beautiful mind in peace.

But all that happiness only lasted for about two weeks, because, as we mentioned earlier . . .

. . . *you-know-who* showed up.

30

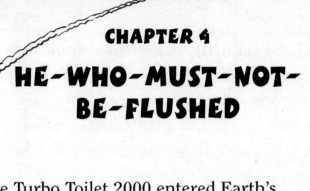

CHAPTER 4

HE-WHO-MUST-NOT-BE-FLUSHED

The Turbo Toilet 2000 entered Earth's atmosphere in a blazing fireball from the sky. His rocket scooter roared over the rooftops of the small Ohio town as the porcelain predator bellowed out an eardrum-crushing taunt, "HEEEEEEEEERE'S JOHNNY!"

Then came the destruction. Buildings collapsed. City buses were thrown through skyscraper windows. Fires raged out of control. The chaos and devastation crippled the town, sent residents running for their lives . . . and annoyed the heck out of one little boy.

Melvin Sneedly had been trying to get some work done in his bedroom laboratory when the attack began. All he needed was one or two more hours of uninterrupted silence to complete his experiment, but the terrible ruckus outside was really getting on his nerves. Melvin marched over to his bedroom window, poked his head out and shouted, "HEY! I'm trying to *WORK*, you idiot! BE *QUIET*!!!"

As you can probably imagine, the Turbo Toilet 2000 didn't take too kindly to being dressed down in such a manner. He swivelled his massive bowl around quickly and glared at Melvin with raging, hard-boiled eyeballs.

"Uh-oh," Melvin gulped.

Suddenly, the Turbo Toilet 2000 leaped at Melvin. The tiny tattletale screamed as the malevolent miscreant chased him down the street, across the city and into the empty, darkened hallways of Jerome Horwitz Elementary School.

Melvin ran upstairs and hid under Mr Krupp's desk while the Turbo Toilet 2000 searched through the classrooms for him. Melvin was in deep trouble. Finally, he *actually* needed Captain Underpants's help, but the Waistband Warrior was nowhere to be found.

"Rats!" said Melvin. "If only I could— *OUCH!*" Melvin's knee was pressing down into something sharp. Carefully, Melvin reached down and pulled the pointy little object out of his knee.

It was a toenail.

Not just any toenail, either. It was one of Mr Krupp's thick, greasy, yellow toenails that he had clipped off the day before he had been whisked away on his journey back through time.

"Ewwww! What a slob!" said Melvin, as
he flicked the toenail away. Then Melvin
thought of something. He knew that Mr
Krupp was also Captain Underpants. That
meant that Mr Krupp's DNA must have
some kind of super-powered element in its
make-up. If Melvin could find a way to extract
the super-powered element from Mr Krupp's
DNA, Melvin could, theoretically, transfer
those super powers to himself!

"Where's that toenail?" cried Melvin.

CHAPTER 5
BIG MELVIN RETURNS

The Turbo Toilet 2000 noisily smashed his way from classroom to classroom, getting closer to Mr Krupp's office with each thundering footstomp. Melvin desperately searched the mangy, orange carpet for Mr Krupp's stinky toenail, digging his fingers deep into the matted shag as the sounds of carnage got louder and louder.

"Where's that toenail?" Melvin screamed.

Finally, Mr Krupp's office door burst
open.

"A-HA!" shouted the Turbo Toilet 2000.
"I'VE GOT YOU NOW, YOU ANNOYING
LITTLE BRAT!" He reached down, grabbed
Melvin by the foot and pulled him towards
his chomping, razor-sharp teeth.

"NOOOOOO," screamed Melvin. "I'M TOO
GIFTED TO DIE! I'M TOO TALENTED! I'M
TOO— *OUCH*!"

38

Once again, Mr Krupp's stinky toenail had lodged its way into Melvin's pasty, freckled skin. But this time, Melvin couldn't have been happier about it. Quickly, he reached back, untied his shoe and slipped his foot out. Then, Melvin jumped out of Mr Krupp's window and slid down the flagpole, with the Turbo Toilet 2000 in hot pursuit.

Fortunately, Melvin's Li'l Scientist Wristwatch had a built-in DNA extractor. Melvin inserted the filthy toenail into his watch and programmed a complete extraction procedure while the Turbo Toilet 2000 chased him back through town.

As Melvin ran screaming, his watch quickly pulverized and sonicated the toenail cells, removed the membrane lipids, proteins and RNA, and purified and isolated a single strand of Mr Krupp's DNA.

When Melvin reached his bedroom laboratory, he quickly fed the results into his Mecha-Computer, which identified the metallo-organic, "super-powered" substance and began replicating it in a saline gel solution. The gel percolated slowly as it oozed into a glass beaker.

"Hurry up, you dumb semi-conservative genome replication device!" shouted Melvin, as the Turbo Toilet 2000 crashed through his bedroom wall.

41

"*Gotcha!*" roared the loathsome lavatory. He scooped Melvin into his gigantic fist as his wet, leathery tongue slid back and forth against his pointed porcelain premolars.

With one final, desperate thrust, Melvin grabbed the beaker and chugged down its green, glowing contents.

The Turbo Toilet 2000 popped Melvin
into his mouth like a cocktail weenie and
started to chew. His ferocious fangs chomped
feverishly, but Melvin was tough and hard
and surprisingly gristly. Then the Turbo
Toilet 2000 struggled to swallow, a task that
he found nearly impossible.

With his gigantic metal fingers, he
reached into his bowl and pulled out a
mucus-covered little boy, who, surprisingly,
didn't have a scratch on him. The Turbo
Toilet 2000 gawked at Melvin in
dumbfounded astonishment.

"You are *so* immature," said Melvin.

CHAPTER 6

SANITIZED
FOR YOUR PROTECTION

Unfortunately, the epic fight that followed was WAY too violent and disturbing to appear in a children's book. The images and descriptions would just be too terrifying. You'd have nightmares for weeks, trust me!

So I have invited a guest illustrator, Timmy Swanson (age four) to draw the action in a style that won't depict too much graphic detail. I've also asked his nana, Gertrude (age seventy-one), to describe the scene in her own, gentle vocabulary.

Take it away, Timmy and Nana!

TODAY'S
SPECIAL
GUESTS

Thank you, dear. Well, let's see what's happening here. What— oh, my. That . . . that's horrible!

It looks like a little boy is— oh, dear. Now what's he doing? Oh, dear me! This certainly is not appropriate at all!

    And now there's a
robot shaped like a— well, I'd rather
not say. He's just doing such dreadful
things, though. And— OH! Oh, my. Say,
what kind of a book is this?

    Oh, for heaven's sake! This is
ridiculous. I've never been so offended
in all my— OH! I've seen just about
enough— OH! OH!!! Oh, dear!

47

Timmy! Stop drawing! Stop drawing this instant!

No, Timmy! No!

CHAPTER 7

THE INCREDIBLY GRAPHIC VIOLENCE CHAPTER, PART 1 (IN FLIP-O-RAMA™)

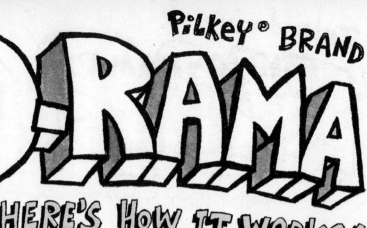

PILKEY® BRAND

:RAMA

HERE'S HOW IT WORKS!

STEP 1
First, place your *left* hand inside the dotted lines marked "LEFT HAND HERE". Hold the book open *flat*.

STEP 2
Grasp the *right-hand* page with your right thumb and index finger (inside the dotted lines marked "RIGHT THUMB HERE").

STEP 3
Now *quickly* flip the right-hand page back and forth until the picture appears to be *animated*.

(For extra fun, try adding your own sound-effects!)

FLIP-O-RAMA 1

(pages 53 and 55)

Remember, flip *only* page 53.
While you are flipping, be sure you
can see the picture on page 53
and the one on page 55.
If you flip quickly, the two
pictures will start to look like
<u>one</u> *animated* picture.

Don't forget to
add your own sound-effects!

LEFT HAND HERE

OH, DEAR!!!

RIGHT
THUMB
HERE

54

OH, DEAR!!!

FLIP-O-RAMA 2

(pages 57 and 59)

Remember, flip *only* page 57.
While you are flipping, be sure you
can see the picture on page 57
and the one on page 59.
If you flip quickly, the two
pictures will start to look like
<u>one</u> *animated* picture.

Don't forget to
add your own sound-effects!

LEFT HAND HERE

OH, MY!!!

RIGHT
THUMB
HERE

OH, MY!!!

FLIP-O-RAMA 3

(pages 61 and 63)

Remember, flip *only* page 61.
While you are flipping, be sure you
can see the picture on page 61
and the one on page 63.
If you flip quickly, the two
pictures will start to look like
<u>one</u> *animated* picture.

Don't forget to
add your own sound-effects!

LEFT HAND HERE

OH,
FOR GOODNESS'
SAKE!!!

61

RIGHT
THUMB
HERE

OH,
FOR GOODNESS'
SAKE!!!

CHAPTER 8

EVERYBODY LOVES MELVIN

When it was all over, the Turbo Toilet 2000 was dead and Melvin Sneedly was a HERO! The mayor had a big parade in honour of Melvin. "Weird Al" Yankovic wrote a song about him. Even the vice president sent a letter of congratulations!

Melvin Sneedly was known throughout the world as the little, super-powered tattletale who saved the world.

"Finally!" said Melvin. "I'm getting the respect I deserve!"

CHAPTER 9

WITH GREAT POWER COMES A GREAT BIG PAIN IN THE HINEY

Melvin enjoyed being a superhero – at first.
It was fun stopping runaway trains, rescuing
lost children and saving people from
burning buildings. Whenever anybody needed
help, all they had to do was lift their heads
to the sky and cry out, "YO! Big Melvin!"
And Big Melvin would drop whatever he was
doing and zip to the scene and save the day.
It was all good, at first . . . until it started
to get bad.

You see, after a while people started to abuse the system. They started crying out "YO! Big Melvin!" all the time, and it got old pretty quickly.

Melvin would drop everything, throw on his cape, fly out the window, zip through the city and arrive at the scene, only to find out that it wasn't an emergency at all. Usually it was just someone who had misplaced her cell phone . . . or a kid who needed help with a video game cheat code . . . or some guy who had accidentally dropped his wallet in the toilet.

It was a complete waste of Melvin's time, and the interruptions were beginning to drive him crazy.

But the final straw came one evening as Melvin was doing a synchrotron radiation experiment with his home-made oscillating-field particle accelerator. Eleven months of research were finally about to pay off. The klystrons and electromagnets began to accelerate the hadrons faster and faster through Melvin's home-made copper cyclone tubing. Soon, Melvin would be the first person on Earth to definitively prove the Higgs boson's existence and solve the mystery of everything.

But then, with his supersonic eardrums, Melvin heard a cry for help from across the city.

Quickly, Melvin shut down his experiment, which caused the particle accelerator to overheat. The resulting explosion blew a hole in his bedroom floor forty feet deep. But Melvin didn't care. Somewhere in the city, a citizen needed his help. So he grabbed his smouldering cape from the pile of ashes that used to be his bedroom closet and flew to the scene of the emergency.

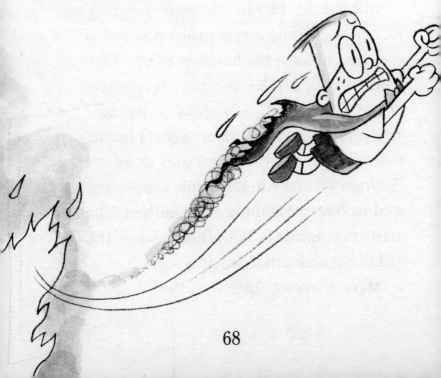

When he arrived, he found a middle-aged woman screaming frantically out her apartment window. "YO! Big Melvin! HELP!!! HELP!!! It's an emergency!!!"

"What's wrong?" Melvin asked desperately.

69

"Do these pants make me look fat?" asked the lady.

CHAPTER 10

IT'S A MAD, MAD, MAD, MAD MELVIN

Melvin was angry. Very, very angry. Since he'd become a superhero, he'd had no time to do his experiments. He'd had no time off, no sleep, no privacy, no time for *anything*. At that moment, Melvin made a decision. He decided, for his own sanity, to quit the superhero business once and for all. But getting *out* was going to be a lot harder than it was getting in. Melvin needed to find a superhero to replace him. So he made up his mind to locate Captain Underpants, bring him back to Piqua and let *him* deal with all the hassles of superherodom.

Finding Captain Underpants, it turns out, wasn't as hard as Melvin had expected. Melvin knew that George and Harold were usually with Captain Underpants, and Sulu the Bionic Hamster was usually with George and Harold.

"So," Melvin concluded, "if I find Sulu, I *should* find Captain Underpants!"

Since Melvin had installed a GPS on Sulu's robotic endoskeleton, all Melvin had to do was run a simple scan on his computer for the GPS device. At first, the scan found nothing. So Melvin broadened his search to include all locations *and all times*. Finally, Melvin's search paid off. He found Sulu's last satellite-reported location, down by the schoolyard, thirty-nine years in the future.

"That wasn't too hard," Melvin sneered. "But bringing them all back to the present will be a little more complicated!"

CHAPTER 11
DARK FORESHADOWS

Melvin went to his garage and climbed into his glow-in-the-dark, time-travelling Robo-Squid suit. Quickly, the suit powered up and started slinking and slithering towards the schoolyard as Melvin began the long journey to bring George, Harold and Captain Underpants back home where they belonged.

After solving some surveillance photo issues at the bank, Melvin zapped himself to the future, fetched everyone and brought them all back one year earlier to the exact time and place where they had departed on their journey in our last book.

George, Harold and Captain Underpants had been through a lot in the past few days, but now it was as if they had never left at all. Everything was just as it had been.

The Turbo Toilet 2000 wouldn't arrive on Earth for another two weeks, so Melvin's future as a superhero would never become reality. And nobody was happier about that than Melvin himself.

"I don't have to be a superhero any more!" cried Melvin happily. "I can finally follow my destiny! Peace and quiet at last!"

"But you still haven't told us why you've brought us back," said George.

"Yeah," said Harold. "What gives?"

"Oh, you'll find out," said Melvin with a foreboding chuckle. "In two weeks, you'll find out!" Melvin unleashed a horrible, villainous laugh as his glow-in-the-dark Robo-Squid suit began to shake and buzz. Soon, he and his tentacled time machine disappeared into a ball of electric light.

CHAPTER 12

HEADIN' HOME

George and Harold had no choice but to take Mr Krupp home. They brought him to his front door, got the key out from behind the bushes and let him inside.

"Go over to the kitchen sink and splash some water on your face," said George.

"Aye, aye, sir!" said Captain Underpants.

He did as he was told, and in no time at all he was back to his grumpy old self.

"I wonder what's going to happen in two weeks," said Harold, as he and George walked home.

"Aw, I'm sure it's no big deal," said George. "If Melvin can handle it, *WE* can handle it!"

Soon, George and Harold were back up
in their tree house. Carefully, they placed
Crackers's eggs on some soft pillows under a
few desk lamps.

"There," said George. "That should keep
them warm and cozy!"

George and Harold were dead tired. They
hadn't slept in over thirty hours, and they'd
been running for their lives most of that time.

"I need a *serious* nap," said Harold, as he settled into his beanbag chair.

"Me, too," said George, as he collapsed into his own beanbag chair. "Saving the world is exhausting!"

"I'm still a little worried about that whole 'two weeks' thing," said Harold. "That sounds really bad!"

"Relax," said George. "There's nothing we can do about it now, anyway."

"Let's try to stay out of trouble for the next two weeks," said Harold. "If the world is going to end, I don't want to be stuck in detention the whole time."

"Aw, don't worry so much," said George. "Besides, how much trouble could we get into in two weeks, anyway?"

80

CHAPTER 13
ELEVEN MINUTES LATER

"GEORGE!"

"HAROLD!!!"

"GET DOWN HERE RIGHT NOW!!!"

George and Harold opened their eyes. Wearily, they stumbled to the tree house door and looked down. George's mum and dad and Harold's mum were all standing down in the yard looking very angry.

"The school called," George's dad said. "They told us that you kids weren't in class today!"

"Uh-oh," said George.

"We're dead," said Harold.

"Would you mind explaining what you've been doing all day?" asked Harold's mum angrily.

George and Harold could hide the truth no longer. They decided to confess everything.

"We couldn't go to school today," said George. "We had to save the Earth from an evil, crazy guy who was riding around in a giant pair of robotic pants."

"Yeah," said Harold.
"We've spent the last day
travelling through time,
running from dinosaurs
and teaching cavemen how
to defend themselves!"

83

"Very funny!" shouted George's dad. "If you kids think you can skip school and goof around all day, you're in for a BIG SURPRISE!"

George and Harold had never seen their parents so angry.

The two boys spent the next five hours mowing lawns, weeding gardens, hoovering houses, washing cars, dusting furniture, cleaning out garages, whitewashing fences, doing dishes, folding laundry and taking out rubbish. It was exhausting work, but it was nothing compared to what was to come next.

CHAPTER 14

WHAT WAS TO COME NEXT

George and Harold had never been so tired
in all their lives. At 9:30 P.M., they grunted
"good night" to each other and limped into
their houses like zombies.

"Would you like a snack, dear?" said Harold's mother.

"No, thanks," he mumbled. He was too tired for a snack. Too tired to take a bath. Too tired to put his pyjamas on or take his shoes off. He didn't even have the energy to turn out his bedroom light. He just collapsed on top of his bed and fell asleep instantly.

Twenty-two seconds later, the telephone rang. It was George.

Harold's mother brought the phone into his room and held it up to his ear. Harold was too tired to even say hello. He just mumbled, "Mmfffff?"

"I just remembered something," said George, panicking. "Tomorrow is *TEST DAY*!!!"

Harold's bloodshot eyes popped open and he sat up straight.

"OH, NO!" Harold cried. "I forgot all about that!"

"Me, too," said George. "We're having major tests in all of our classes tomorrow. We're gonna have to stay up all night long and study!!!"

CHAPTER 15

TO THINE OWN SELF BE TRUANT

When the sun rose the next day, George and Harold were still going through their spelling checklists. George was almost done studying. Harold still had to read forty-four pages of his natural history textbook.

"Breakfast is ready!" shouted George's dad from downstairs.

George stumbled down exhaustedly and tried to smoosh some waffles into his mouth. He missed.

Meanwhile, Harold was sitting at his breakfast table in a burned-out stupor, buttering his cereal and pouring milk on his toast.

"Did you get *any* sleep at all last night?" asked Harold's mum.

"OK," Harold answered.

Harold's answer didn't make any sense, but it was the best he could do under the circumstances.

89

Before long, George and Harold were ready for school.

They met up, as they did every school day, in George's front yard.

"Are you ready for all of our big tests today?" asked George droopily.

"Pretty good," said Harold. He was so tired he couldn't even answer a simple question from his best friend correctly. How was he going to manage a day's worth of tests?

"Let's get this over with," George moaned.

"Wait!" said Harold. "I want to check on Crackers's eggs before we go to school."

Harold wobbled to George's garden and hoisted himself up the ladder to the tree house.

"Hurry up!" said George.

Harold did not answer.

"Hey!" shouted George. "We're gonna be late!"

Harold did not come down.

George climbed up the steps and peeked inside the tree house.

It was just as he had expected. Harold had fallen asleep at their desk.

"Hey, Harold," said George, shaking his friend's shoulder. "Wake up, man! We're gonna be late for our tests!"

"Just five minutes," moaned Harold. "I just need to sleep for five minutes. *PLEASE!!!*"

"Well, OK," said George. "But not a minute longer!"

George took his backpack off and set it against the tree house door. Then he plopped down in his beanbag chair and looked at his pocket watch.

7:53 A.M.

The second hand was ticking by awfully slowly. "I'm just going to close my eyes for a second," said George. "Just for a few seconds. . ."

That afternoon, George yawned and stretched as he rolled over in his beanbag chair. He glanced at his pocket watch again.

4:41 P.M.

George closed his eyes and went back to sleep. Suddenly, his eyes shot open.

"OH! NOOOOO!" George screamed. Harold awoke with a jump. "WE FELL ASLEEP!" George cried. "WE SLEPT THROUGH SCHOOL!!! WE SLEPT THROUGH OUR TESTS!!! WE SLEPT THROUGH EVERY-THING!!!"

"Oh, *NOOO*!" Harold wailed. "We're *DEAD*, man! GAME OVER!!!"

George and Harold peeked out their tree house window. Harold's mum was out in her garden. She was whistling a cheerful tune.

"That's strange," said Harold. "Why didn't the school call her and tell her we were absent?"

"I have no idea," said George.

95

George and Harold climbed down
from the tree house and walked over to
the garden.

"How was school today?" asked Harold's
mum.

"Oh, same as always, I guess," said
Harold. He really *was* guessing.

George's mum heard them talking and
came over.

"You didn't miss school today, did you?"
asked George's mum.

"Ummm . . . nope," said George.
Technically, George was telling the truth.
He hadn't really *missed* school at all.

96

CHAPTER 16
SUPER-SECRET TEST DAY

The next day when George and Harold
arrived at school, Mr Krupp was
OVERJOYED to see them. He met them
at the front door, shook their hands
enthusiastically and gave them both big,
sweaty hugs.

"This can't be good," George said.

"You're wrong," said Mr Krupp. "It's
the BEST DAY EVER! It's the day I've been
waiting for since I met you two horrible
people. Let's all go to my office, shall we?
I've got refreshments!"

As they walked down the long hallway
towards Mr Krupp's office, several teachers
patted Mr Krupp on the back and
congratulated him. The entire school staff
seemed elated.

"We're doomed," said Harold.

When they finally got to Mr Krupp's office, he plopped down into his chair and spun around a few times, giggling with glee.

After a few minutes, George started to become impatient.

"I thought you said there were going to be refreshments," George said.

"NOT FOR YOU!!!" shouted Mr Krupp angrily, as he slammed his fist on his desk. He opened his drawer, pulled out a warm diet soda and popped it open. Then he leaned back in his chair and sipped loudly as he chuckled to himself. "I just want to soak this moment in," he said with delight, as fizzy, brown phosphoric acid dribbled down his chins.

"You boys have REALLY messed up this time." Mr Krupp laughed. "You skipped school on Super-Secret Test Day!"

"*Super-Secret* Test Day?" said Harold. "What does *that* mean?"

"I thought you'd never ask," Mr Krupp said gleefully. "You see, I've been looking for a way to separate you two kids for years now, but I never figured out how to do it until yesterday. Then it came to me in a flash of inspiration. SUPER-SECRET TEST DAY!"

"What's so *secret* about it?" asked George.

"You should be asking, 'What's so *SUPER* about it?'" said Mr Krupp joyfully. "Because it just might be the crowning achievement of my entire career!"

George and Harold looked at each other nervously. Suddenly, the door opened and the school's math teacher, Miss Calculator, entered the room. She sneered down at George and Harold and poked her tongue out at them as she walked by. "Here are the figures you asked for," she said, handing Mr Krupp a large manila envelope.

"Thanks, Anita," Mr Krupp said. He smelled the envelope like he was admiring the aroma of a gourmet meal. "It's a real shame you boys missed school yesterday," Mr Krupp said. "Your teachers *hated* to do it, but they had to give you both *ZEROES* on all of your tests!!!"

"But we studied really hard," said Harold. "Can't we take make-up tests?"

"No, no, no, no, no," Mr Krupp said, grinning evilly from ear to ear. "There will be no make-up tests!"

"Don't worry, Harold," said George. "We'll do really good on our final exams this year! We can bring our grades back up."

"Final exams have been cancelled for this year," said Mr Krupp cheerfully. "Isn't that wonderful news? You and all your classmates will get seven more weeks of school with no homework, no quizzes and no studying. Your grades for the whole school year have already been calculated."

"Oh, NO," said George. "We're – we're going to *flunk the fourth grade*?!!?"

"Actually, it's *worse* than that," said Mr Krupp, his yellow teeth glistening in a grin so wide it seemed to stretch beyond the boundaries of his face. "Normally, you wouldn't get this information until summer vacation begins, but I thought I'd be nice and show you your grades early. Isn't that fun?!!?"

He opened the manila envelope and slid two report cards towards George and Harold. Quickly, the boys opened them up and scanned through them. George's final grade for the year was 62.7 per cent. A terrible grade, to be sure, but still a *passing* grade. George would move on to fifth grade next year. Harold, whose grades were not quite as good as George's, wasn't so lucky. Harold's final grade was 59.7 per cent. Harold had failed.

"Oh, NO!" Harold moaned, as his eyes began to fill with tears. "I'm going to flunk the fourth grade!"

"Yeah, ain't that too bad?" said Mr Krupp with a delighted twinkle in his eyes. He looked up at Miss Calculator, and they both burst into fits of laughter.

"There's nothing you can do about it, either," Miss Calculator sneered. "You two brats will be in different grades next year. You'll never see each other in school any more! You'll have different teachers, classes . . . and *different friends*!"

CHAPTER 17

THE IDEA

"I can't believe they're going to separate us," said Harold, as the boys walked home from school that afternoon.

George said nothing. He was thinking. He KNEW there was a way to solve this problem.

"I can't believe I have to spend an *EXTRA YEAR* at that school, too," Harold moaned, trying not to cry. "The worst part is that I actually studied! *I know this stuff!* I could have probably gotten *straight Bs* if I had taken those tests yesterday!"

"THAT'S IT!" cried George confidently. "We can fix this!"

"But *HOW*?" said Harold. "They won't let us take make-up tests!"

"Who says we have to take make-up tests?" George replied. "Let's take the *real* tests!"

Harold looked suspicious. "What do you mean?" he asked.

"Melvin said he kept his time-travelling squid thingy in his garage, right?" said George. "Let's borrow it and go back in time to yesterday morning. Then we can take those tests like we were supposed to. Problem solved!"

"No *WAY*!" Harold protested. "Whenever we travel around in time, bad stuff happens!"

"What could be worse than being in different grades next year?" George countered. "Do you really want to spend an extra *YEAR* at that school?"

Harold didn't have an argument for that.

"Besides," said George, "we're only going back in time one day. How could anything bad happen in just one day?"

"I guess you're right," said Harold.

George and Harold turned around and headed over to Melvin's house. Luckily, Melvin's garage door was open. Cautiously, the two boys sneaked inside and looked around. And there, standing in the corner beside a box of Langstrom seven-inch gangly wrenches was the glow-in-the-dark, time-travelling Robo-Squid suit.

"We shouldn't be doing this," Harold whispered. "We're trespassing – and stealing!"

"Hey, Melvin started this whole mess," George reminded Harold. "We're just fixing it! Besides, we're not stealing. We're just *borrowing*."

Against his better judgement, Harold helped hoist George up into the cockpit. Suddenly, the Robo-Squid suit powered up and began to glow. A few moments later, the controls were all set.

"OK," said George. "Let's go back in time and take those dumb tests!" He picked Harold up with one of his glowing tentacles, took a few steps forward and pressed the "Start" button.

The glow-in-the-dark, time-travelling
Robo-Squid suit began shaking and
sputtering as it zipped backwards in time
thirty-two hours. A blinding ball of light
flashed suddenly, and George and Harold
arrived bright and early yesterday morning,
just in time for school.

As Harold helped George climb out of the cockpit, he noticed that there were now *TWO* glow-in-the-dark, time-travelling Robo-Squid suits.

"Hey," said Harold. "How come there are *TWO* glow-in-the-dark, time-travelling Robo-Squid suits?"

"Hmmmm," said George. "I guess that one in the corner is the one from yesterday. When we went back in time, we created a duplicate time machine."

"Oh," said Harold. "Melvin should thank us!"

"Yeah," said George. "That was very thoughtful of us."

George and Harold ran back through town as fast as they could. Soon they were scrambling up the steps of Jerome Horwitz Elementary School.

"This feels weird," said George. "I've never been so happy to go to school before."

"Or to take tests!" said Harold.

And indeed, it was a happy school day for George and Harold. They took all of their tests, did pretty well on most of them and never had to deal with anything *Super* or *Secret* again. At least not until that afternoon.

CHAPTER 18

OUR DOPPEL GÄNG

That afternoon, when George and Harold got home, they climbed up to their tree house to check on Crackers's eggs. George tried to push the door open, but something was in the way.

"Hey, there's a backpack blocking the door," said George. He reached in and pulled it towards him. "This — this looks like *MY* backpack!"

"What's going on up there?" asked Harold, as George rummaged through the backpack.

"My papers! My books! My lunch from yesterday!" said George. "This *IS* my backpack!"

"It can't be," said Harold. "You're wearing your backpack!"

George pushed the tree house door open and looked inside.

"Oh, *NOOOOO*!" said George.

Harold climbed up next to George and looked inside the tree house. There, sleeping at the table, was Harold himself. And next to him, sprawled out and snoring on his beanbag chair, was George.

"I *TOLD* you something bad would happen!" cried Harold.

"Shhhhh!" said George. "Don't wake us up!"

"I don't understand," Harold whispered. "How come *WE'RE* here?"

"Well, it kind of makes sense," said George. "We just went back in time to yesterday, right?"

"Right," said Harold.

"Well, where were *we* yesterday?" asked George.

"We were right up here in the tree house, sleeping and . . . Oh, I get it," said Harold. "This is us from yesterday!"

"Yeah," said George. "Remember how we accidentally created an extra Robo-Squid suit?"

"Mmm-hmmm," said Harold.

"I guess we accidentally created an extra George and Harold, too."

"Perfect," said Harold sarcastically.

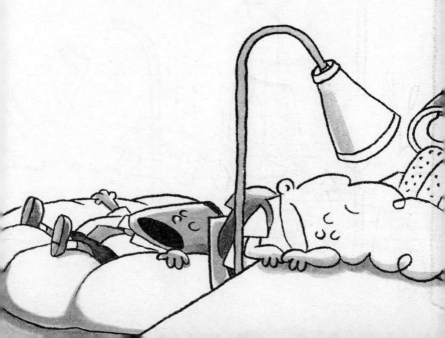

CHAPTER 19

THE PACT

While yesterday's George and Harold slept, George and Harold tried to figure out what to do next.

"How are we going to explain this to our parents?" asked Harold.

"How are we going to explain this to *ourselves*?" asked George.

Yesterday George yawned and stretched as he rolled over in his beanbag chair. He glanced at his pocket watch, then closed his eyes to go back to sleep. Suddenly, his eyes shot open.

"OH! NOOOOO!" Yesterday George screamed. Yesterday Harold awoke with a jump. "WE FELL ASLEEP!" Yesterday George cried. "WE SLEPT THROUGH SCHOOL!!! WE SLEPT THROUGH OUR TESTS!!! WE SLEPT THROUGH— *Hey, who are you guys*?"

Yesterday Harold rubbed his eyes and looked at his twin. "I must be dreaming," he said. "Either that or I'm seeing double!"

"Well," said George, "it's a long story." He and Harold told their yesterday selves what had happened, and quickly caught them both up on the events of the past three and a half chapters.

"*Now* what are we supposed to do?" said Yesterday George.

"We can't tell our parents," said Harold.

"But where are we all going to sleep?" asked Yesterday Harold.

"And how are we all going to get enough food?" said Yesterday George.

"And clean clothes?" said Harold.

Everyone was beginning to panic except for George, who had been deep in thought for a while. George didn't seem worried at all. In fact, a devilish grin was beginning to spread across his face.

"You know," George said, "maybe we're looking at this the wrong way. Maybe this is a *good* thing!"

"A *GOOD* thing?" cried Yesterday Harold incredulously.

"Yeah," said George. "We've always said there's never enough time to do what we *want* to do. So let's take shifts. Me and Harold will start going to school and doing our homework on *even* numbered days, and you guys will go to school and do homework on *odd* numbered days."

"Yeah, but what'll *WE* do while you guys are at school?" asked Yesterday George.

"Whatever you want," said George. "Hang out in the tree house! Play video games! Make comics! Watch monster movies! It doesn't matter. You guys get to relax and take the day off *every other day*!"

"I get it," said Yesterday George, smiling devilishly. "Then YOU guys can take the day off while *WE'RE* at school and stuff."

"Yeah!" said George. "Just think of the possibilities!"

"I don't know," said Harold and Yesterday Harold at the same time.

"Don't worry," said George. "It'll be GREAT! We'll have TWICE as much fun as normal, and only half the work!"

"Yeah!" said Yesterday George. "What could possibly go wrong?"

CHAPTER 20
SHIFT WORKERS

Since today was an even numbered weekday, it was decided that Yesterday George and Yesterday Harold would go to school the next day. So the Yesterday boys said goodbye and headed down to their respective homes to eat, do homework and prepare for the next day at school.

George and Harold were ready for a night off. Harold grabbed a stack of comics, George turned on a monster movie and the two friends settled into their beanbag chairs for some well-deserved R and R.

Fortunately, they had enough juice boxes, Zing Zong Cupcakes and Fruit Rollie-Flops to last them for a while.

Around 9:30 P.M., George called Piqua Pizza Palace and ordered two calzones, some cheesy breadsticks and two 2-litre bottles of ice-cold soft drink.

The boys waited in George's driveway so the delivery guy wouldn't ring the doorbell.

Soon, the two friends were enjoying the finest carbohydrates money could buy, in the quiet comfort of their cozy tree house.

"This is the life," said George, as he pressed "Play" on the horror movie masterpiece *Baby Blob 2: The Squishening*.

Harold, who was usually cautious in situations like this, had to admit it: This was indeed the life.

CHAPTER 21

PROBLEMS

The next morning, George and Harold woke up late. "Ahhh, it's nice to sleep in for a change, isn't it?" said George.

"Yeah," said Harold. "But I gotta pee."

This was something that George and Harold hadn't thought about. Usually, they would just climb down the ladder and run to their houses to use the bathroom. But George's and Harold's mums both worked from home, and they would not be happy to see the boys running in and out of the house on a school day.

Fortunately, empty 2-litre bottles come in very handy for such situations. But as they poured the contents of their emergency urinals out the window, both boys knew this solution wouldn't work for long.

"Our food is running low," said Harold, "and I spent all of my allowance on those calzones last night."

"No problem," said George. "We'll make a comic book, sell it on the playground at school and use the money to buy all the junk we need! We can even buy one of those portable camping toilet thingies!"

"But we're not supposed to go to school today," said Harold.

"Actually, we're not supposed to go to our *classes* today!" George clarified. "As long as we're never in the same place as our doubles, we should be fine."

So George and Harold cleared a space at their desk and began working on their newest comic book. It was called:

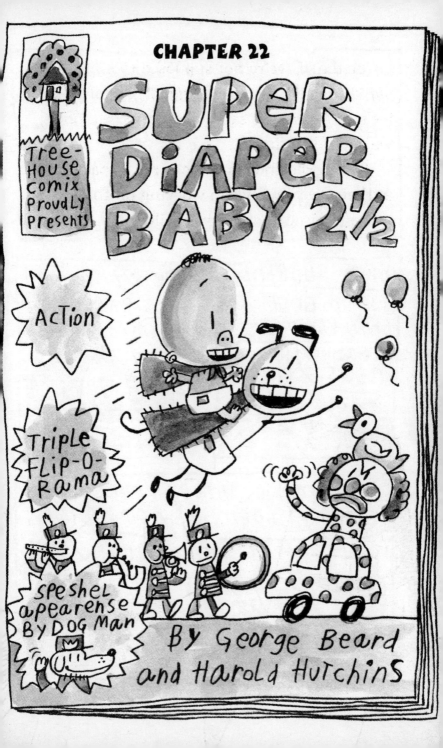

We've got to be very care-full!!!

Petey is going to try and trick us!

we must be on the lookout for his evil ways!

2 Seconds Later...

DING DONG!

OH! I wonder who that could be?

Yes?

HELLO! I'm P.T. Duckhat.

DOG MAN had a Little itch.

His FLeas were white as snow.

and every-where the ROBO-BABY went....

Right Thum Here.

DOG MAN had a Little itch.	
His FLeas were white as snow.	
and everywhere the ROBO-BABY went....	

CHAPTER 23

DREAM A LITTLE DREAM OF US

"Hey, that comic turned out pretty good," said Harold.

"Yeah, not too shabby!" said George. "Let's go to school and make copies of it."

"But what if somebody sees us?" said Harold.

"Don't worry," said George. "I've got it all figured out!"

So George and Harold headed to school and sneaked into the office. In no time at all, they were running off copies of their new comic book and stapling them together. Things were going very well until the school secretary, Miss Anthrope, came back from her lunch break.

"What are you kids doing in my office?!!?" Miss Anthrope yelled.

"We're *not* in your office," said George with a mischievous smile. "You're dreaming!"

"Dreaming?" said Miss Anthrope.

"Yeah! And I can prove it," said George. "Just call our teacher, Ms Ribble, on the intercom. She'll tell you that we're both in class right now."

"In *class*?" said Miss Anthrope.

"Yep," said George. "Obviously, we can't be in two places at the same time, so this *HAS* to be a dream, right?"

Miss Anthrope was suspicious. She grabbed the microphone on the intercom and contacted Ms Ribble's room.

"Ms Ribble?" she said. "Where are George and Harold right now?"

"Why, they're right here in my classroom," Ms Ribble replied through the speaker.

"Oh, *REALLY*?" said Miss Anthrope.

"Of course," said Ms Ribble. "They've been here all day."

Miss Anthrope was stumped. Then she got a sneaky idea. "All right," she said. "If they're *really* in your classroom, then send them both to the office right now!"

"OK," said Ms Ribble.

Miss Anthrope turned and looked at George and Harold with a yellowish, snarly grin. "I don't know what kind of trick you kids are trying to pull," she said, "but you can't fool me!"

Suddenly, Yesterday George and Yesterday Harold walked into the office. Miss Anthrope looked at them and screamed. Then she looked at George and Harold and screamed again. Her head made a swishing sound as it swivelled back and forth between George and Harold, and Yesterday George and Yesterday Harold.

"See?" said George. "I *told* you this was a dream."

"You're – you're *RIGHT*!" cried Miss Anthrope. "It all seems so vivid! But I *MUST* be dreaming!"

"Of course you are," said George. "And why should you waste a perfectly good dream hanging around the office?"

"That's a good point!" said Miss Anthrope. "And why bother wearing such tight, restricting clothes? After all, it's MY DREAM! I can do whatever I want!"

"Now, wait a minute," said Harold.

But it was too late. Miss Anthrope hoisted
her dress over her head, ripped it off and
threw it out the window.

"Wheeeeee!" she yelled. "Dreaming is
FUN!" Then she ran away laughing her head
off and slammed the office door behind her.

"What are you guys doing here?!!?" said
Yesterday George sternly. "This is *OUR* day to
be at school!"

"We ran out of food, and we needed to buy
some supplies," said George. "So we made a
new comic to sell on the playground."

146

Yesterday Harold walked over to the copy machine and inspected the new comic. "How many did you make?" he asked.

"About two hundred," said Harold.

"Well, leave them with us," said Yesterday Harold. "We'll sell them at break time today and bring the money to the tree house after school."

"Yeah," said George. "But we—"

"*You guys need to get out of here!*" Yesterday George interrupted. "If anybody else catches us together, we'll ALL be in BIG TROUBLE!"

"All right, all right," said George.

"GET OUT, *NOW*!" shouted Yesterday George angrily.

"*ALL RIGHT!*" said George. "*Gee whiz!*"

Yesterday George and Yesterday Harold
scooped up the comics in their arms and left
the office in a huff.

"Man," said George. "Today was supposed
to be *our* day to have fun! But we won't let
us!"

"I know," said Harold. "Who do we think
we are?"

"We can't tell us what to do!" said George.
"I'm not the boss of me!"

"Me, neither," said Harold. "I'm going to
do what I want, even if I don't want me to!"

"That's tellin' yourself!" said George.

CHAPTER 24
TWIN PRANKS

George and Harold went out into the hallway and started switching the letters around on a bulletin board.

Soon they were spotted by two teachers.

"Hey!" Mr Meaner barked. "What do you kids think you're doing?"

"Actually, we're not doing anything," said George. "You guys are dreaming!"

It took even less effort to persuade
Mr Meaner and Miss Labler that *they* were
dreaming, too. Once they looked through Ms
Ribble's classroom window and saw Yesterday
George and Yesterday Harold sitting in their
seats, they were convinced.

"There can't be TWO Georges and TWO
Harolds!" cried Mr Meaner. "So this *HAS* to
be a dream!"

"That's right," said Harold. "You can do
ANYTHING you want! Just don't take off
your clothes and—"

151

"Oops, too late."

Mr Meaner tore off down the hallway
laughing like a crazy person and singing "Itsy
Bitsy Spider" at the top of his lungs. Miss Labler
headed straight for the teachers' lounge, where
she yanked open the refrigerator and started
stuffing her face with everyone's lunches.

"HALLELUJAH!" she cried. "I can eat
anything I want and not gain weight!"

"Hey! That's *OUR* food!" cried Mr Rected.

"No, it's not," giggled Miss Labler. "This is
a dream! Check it out for yourselves!"

153

With a mouth full of tuna salad and chocolate chip cookies, she led them all down to Ms Ribble's classroom window. Soon they were convinced, too.

George and Harold watched in shock as teacher after teacher started going crazy. Mr Meaner brought in a garden hose and started spraying down the hallway with soapy water. "IT'S THE WORLD'S BIGGEST SLIP 'N' SLIDE!" he cried.

By the time Mr Krupp came out of the teachers' bathroom, nearly all of the staff, including the caretaker, the lunch ladies and most of the parent volunteers, were laughing their heads off, throwing soap suds at each other and slipping and sliding down the hallway in their giant underwear.

"WHAT THE HECK IS GOING ON HERE?!!?" Mr Krupp screamed.

"It's the greatest dream ever!" cried Ms Dayken.

She brought Mr Krupp over to Ms
Ribble's classroom window and showed him
the proof. But when Mr Krupp saw that there
were now *two* Georges and *two* Harolds, his
reaction was a bit different from the other
adults' reactions. He tried to speak. He tried
to convince himself that he was dreaming.
He tried to say SOMETHING . . . but all that
came out was "B-B-Bubba bobba hob-hobba-
hobba wah-wah."

CHAPTER 25

TWELVE DAYS OF CHAOS

It didn't take long before the cops showed up. They attempted to restore order, but things didn't go very well.

"We can either do this the easy way, or the hard way!" shouted Officer McWiggly.

"Let's do it the *FUN* way!" cried Miss Fitt, as she yanked Officer McWiggly's pants down around his ankles.

"I've got a good idea," said George.

"What?" asked Harold.

"RUN!" said George.

By the time it was all over, the entire staff of Jerome Horwitz Elementary School was in prison.

The charges ranged from indecent exposure and resisting arrest to reckless endangerment and *pantsing* a police officer.

The cops didn't quite know what to do with Mr Krupp, though. He hadn't really done anything wrong. He'd just stood there in the same spot for hours and hours, saying "B-B-Bubba bobba hob-hobba-hobba wah-wah" over and over and *OVER* again.

So it was decided that he should be admitted into the Piqua Valley Home for the Reality-Challenged, where he remained, unchanged, for nearly two weeks.

George and Harold and their twins spent the next twelve days being *VERY* careful.

"Great job!" shouted Yesterday George angrily. "Our teachers are in jail, and Mr Krupp is in the goof house. These past two weeks have been a total disaster!"

"Two weeks?" said Harold inquisitively.

"Yeah," Yesterday George continued. "In the past two weeks you guys have—"

"No, wait," Harold interrupted. "Wasn't something *BAD* supposed to happen in two weeks?"

George, Yesterday George and Yesterday Harold all thought back to Melvin Sneedly's cryptic warning in chapter 11.

"Oh, yeah," they all said simultaneously.

The four boys looked around them. They checked the horizon. They sniffed the air. They put their ears to the floor and listened. Nothing. There was no sign of any trouble.

"Huh!" said George. "I guess nothing bad is going to happen after all!"

Suddenly, a fireball shot out from behind the clouds. Then came an echoing, eardrum-piercing sound of relentless terror. It was a laugh. A horrifying, sinister, stomach-churning laugh that the boys had not heard for many months. A laugh that they'd hoped they would never hear again.

"Uh-oh," said the Georges.

"We're doomed!" cried the Harolds.

CHAPTER 26
HEEEEEEEEERE'S JOHNNY!

The Turbo Toilet 2000 zipped across the rooftops in his home-made rocket scooter, laughing ferociously as a trail of choking smoke filled the afternoon sky.

Everyone screamed. Everyone cried. Everyone hid.

Everyone, that is, except for George and Harold and their dreadfully distressed duplicates.

The four boys ran as fast as they could to the Piqua Valley Home for the Reality-Challenged.

There was only one person who could stop this horrifying beast, and he was locked away in the goof house.

The four boys dashed through the sanitarium's front door and slid across the freshly waxed floor to the reception desk.

"We need to see Mr Krupp," cried George, almost out of breath. "He's a patient here."

"Sorry," said the nurse. "But patients can't have visitors without a doctor's permission."

"But he can save the world," cried Harold. "He's Captain Underpants!"

"Sure he is," said the nurse sarcastically. "Listen, bub: We currently have *nine* patients who claim to be Captain Underpants. We also have four Wonder Women, seven Albert Einsteins and one Elvis Presley!"

"Well, can we at least talk to him?" asked Yesterday Harold.

"No!" said the nurse. "Nobody talks to *The King*."

"NOT ELVIS," said George angrily. "MR KRUPP!"

"Oh," said the nurse. "I'm sorry. But *NO!*"

"Rats," cried Yesterday Harold. "Captain Underpants is stuck in the goof house!"

"*We* can't bust him out," said George, "but I know somebody who CAN. Follow me!" Frantically, the boys ran back across the city.

CHAPTER 27
DISGUISE CRAZY!

George had an idea, and he needed every-one's help to pull it off.

Harold grabbed some cardboard boxes from his garage. George found some white spray paint in his garage. Yesterday George and Yesterday Harold each grabbed a barbecue grill from their gardens.

With a little ingenuity and a lot of duct tape, the four boys constructed two surprisingly convincing Talking Toilet costumes.

George and Harold climbed into the boxes and wheeled themselves awkwardly into town. Soon they came face-to-face with the Turbo Toilet 2000.

"Uh, yum, yum, eat 'em up," said George, opening and closing the barbecue grill lid with every syllable.

"Yeah, eat 'em up and stuff," said Harold, doing the same thing with his lid.

"Hey," cried the Turbo Toilet 2000. "I thought you guys were *dead*!"

"I'm not *quite* dead," said George. "It's just a flush wound."

"Yeah, me, too," said Harold.

"Good!" said the Turbo Toilet 2000. "You can help me look for those two kids who messed up all of our plans a few months ago."

"Um, OK," said George. "But what about that bald guy with the cape and the underwear?"

"I'll get him later!" said the Turbo Toilet 2000. "First I want to find those two meddling kids!"

"I really think you should find that underwear guy first," said Harold.

"Yeah," said George. "He said some really mean things about you."

"OH, HE DID, DID HE?" shouted the Turbo Toilet 2000. "What did he say?!!?"

"Ummm. . ." said George. "He said you're so fat, you have to put your belt on with a boomerang!"

"Yeah," said Harold, "and you're so dumb, you tried to conserve toilet paper by using both sides."

"ENOUGH!" screamed the Turbo Toilet 2000. "WHERE IS HE?!!?"

"Right this way," said Harold.

CHAPTER 28

ONE SMASHED INTO THE CUCKOO'S NEST

The Turbo Toilet 2000 followed George and Harold back to the sanitarium. He marched through the front doors and headed towards the restricted area. The nurses screamed and ran for safety.

Quickly, George grabbed the intercom, turned up the volume and started snapping his fingers into the microphone.

The sounds of finger snapping echoed through the hallways of the Piqua Valley Home for the Reality-Challenged as the Turbo Toilet 2000 crashed from room to room. Mr Krupp, who had been comatose for nearly two weeks, suddenly began to change. First, a mischievous twinkle gleamed in his eyes. Then, a giant smile spread across his face. Suddenly, he ripped off his straitjacket, threw off his pyjamas and grabbed a curtain from a nearby window.

173

Captain Underpants was back, and the battle of the century was about to begin.

CHAPTER 29

THE INCREDIBLY GRAPHIC VIOLENCE CHAPTER, PART 2 (IN FLIP-O-RAMA™)

FLIP-O-RAMA 4

(pages 177 and 179)

Remember, flip *only* page 177.
While you are flipping, be sure you
can see the picture on page 177
and the one on page 179.
If you flip quickly, the two
pictures will start to look like
<u>one</u> *animated* picture.

Don't forget to
add your own sound-effects!

LEFT HAND HERE

HELLO, IT'S NICE
TO BEAT YOU!

177

RIGHT
THUMB
HERE

RIGHT
INDEX
FINGER
HERE

HELLO, IT'S NICE
TO BEAT YOU!

FLIP-O-RAMA 5

(pages 181 and 183)

Remember, flip *only* page 181.
While you are flipping, be sure you
can see the picture on page 181
and the one on page 183.
If you flip quickly, the two
pictures will start to look like
<u>one</u> *animated* picture.

Don't forget to
add your own sound-effects!

LEFT HAND HERE

SPANK YOU
VERY MUCH!

RIGHT
THUMB
HERE

SPANK YOU
VERY MUCH!

FLIP-O-RAMA 6

(pages 185 and 187)

Remember, flip *only* page 185.
While you are flipping, be sure you
can see the picture on page 185
and the one on page 187.
If you flip quickly, the two
pictures will start to look like
<u>one</u> *animated* picture.

Don't forget to
add your own sound-effects!

LEFT HAND HERE

ALL'S SWELL
THAT ENDS SWELL!

185

RIGHT
THUMB
HERE

186

ALL'S SWELL
THAT ENDS SWELL!

CHAPTER 30

TEARS OF A COMMODE

"Let that be a lesson to you," said Captain Underpants gallantly, as the Turbo Toilet 2000 cried and cried.

"Well," said George, "I'm glad that's over with!"

"Yeah," said Harold. "That ended up being a lot easier than I thought it would be!"

At that precise moment, a single teardrop
from the quivering eyeballs of the Turbo
Toilet 2000 flew through the air and landed
on Captain Underpants's face. *Splash!*
Suddenly, our hero's expression began to
change. The sparkle disappeared from his
eyes, his posture deflated and his goofy grin
morphed into a scowling grimace.

"What the heck is going on here?!!?" Mr
Krupp yelled.

"Uh-oh," said Harold.

189

Mr Krupp turned and saw the ginormous
Turbo Toilet 2000 blubbering behind him.
"AAAAAUGH!" the frightened principal
shrieked. "IT'S A MONSTER!!!" And he ran
away screaming his head off.

The Turbo Toilet 2000 wasn't sure what was going on, but he decided to chase Mr Krupp and see what happened. Soon, the leviathan lavatory cornered Mr Krupp and scooped him up in his mighty robotic fist.

"I give up!" cried Mr Krupp. "I surrender! Please don't hurt me!"

"Gee," said the Turbo Toilet 2000. "That ended up being a lot easier than I thought it would be! Now I just need to find those two annoying kids!"

Mr Krupp perked up a little. "Er, what two annoying kids?" he asked.

"Well," said the Turbo Toilet 2000, "one of them had a flat-top and a tie, and the other one wore a T-shirt and had a bad haircut!"

"Hey, I know those kids!" said Mr Krupp excitedly. "I even know where they live!"

"Really?" said the Turbo Toilet 2000. "Then what are we waiting for? Come on, my two toilet minions. Behold, my tyrannical retaliation is at hand!"

Mr Krupp pointed the way, and the Turbo Toilet 2000 marched off towards George's and Harold's houses.

"Uh-oh," said George.

"We're doomed again," said Harold.

CHAPTER 31

THE RE-RETALIATION

The Turbo Toilet 2000 marched to George's and Harold's houses, smashing through buildings, pushing over cars and leaving a smouldering path of destruction behind him. George and Harold tried to keep up, but the Turbo Toilet 2000 left them trailing behind.

"Oh, NO!" cried Harold. "He's heading for our houses, and there's no way to warn ourselves!"

It didn't matter, however, because Yesterday George and Yesterday Harold could hear the Turbo Toilet 2000 coming from miles away.

"I think he's heading straight for us," cried Yesterday George.

"But how would he know where to find us?" asked Yesterday Harold.

"Turn left at Vine Street," said Mr Krupp. "The kids live on this block. I'll bet they're hiding up in that tree house of theirs!"

Yesterday George and Yesterday Harold saw the Turbo Toilet 2000 heading for their garden. They could feel the Earth shake under each stomp of his massive, metal feet. Yesterday George locked the door to the tree house. Yesterday Harold hid under the desk.

"OK," said Mr Krupp. "I've led you to those two kids you were looking for. Can I go now?"

"Sure," said the Turbo Toilet 2000. "You can go *right in here*!" He shoved the screaming principal into his mouth and flushed his little handle. Mr Krupp shrieked in terror as he spun around in a swirling whirlpool of saliva. Then the Turbo Toilet 2000 swallowed hard, and Mr Krupp was flushed away with a gurgling *glug, glug, glug*.

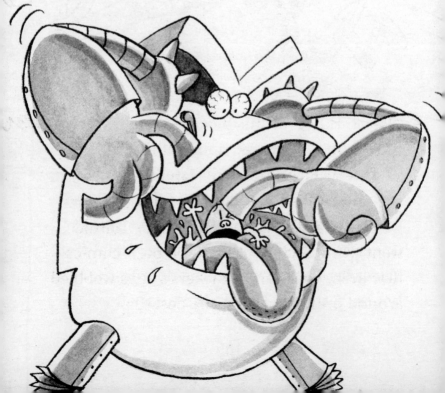

The Turbo Toilet 2000 slammed against the tree with his massive, metallic shoulder. Yesterday George and Yesterday Harold went flying. The bookshelf fell over, comics flew everywhere and Crackers's eggs wobbled around precariously on the desktop.

"GET DOWN HERE, YOU MEDDLING KIDS!" screamed the Turbo Toilet 2000, as he smashed into the tree once more. Yesterday George and Yesterday Harold went flying again. The three eggs teetered perilously back and forth at the edge of the table.

"I'M WARNING YOU!!!" cried the Turbo Toilet 2000. "GIVE UP NOW AND I WON'T MAKE YOU SUFFER!" He ploughed into the tree a third time. This time, the window smashed, the TV toppled over and Crackers's eggs flew off of the table.

Yesterday George and Yesterday Harold
leaped for the eggs.

"NOOOOOOOO!" cried Yesterday Harold,
as the three purple-and-orange-speckled eggs
flew through the air. They hit the floor and
shattered with a terrible crash.

CHAPTER 32

SURPRISE, SURPRISE, SURPRISE!

As the tree house swayed violently from side to side, Yesterday George and Yesterday Harold sifted frantically through the broken eggshell fragments. Suddenly, Yesterday Harold's hand felt something warm and fuzzy. Carefully, he pulled it out of the broken eggshell pieces.

It was a . . . a . . . Yesterday Harold wasn't quite sure *what* it was.

"What the heck is this thing?" cried Yesterday Harold, as the tiny fuzzy creature wrapped its wings around him and looked up lovingly into his eyes.

Yesterday George pulled two more fuzzy winged creatures out of the shell fragments and stared at them in disbelief.

"This – *this can't be*," he cried.

The tree house shook wildly, and Yesterday George and Yesterday Harold went flying again. The three tiny creatures happily wiggled their way up to the boys' faces and started licking their cheeks.

The Turbo Toilet 2000 climbed up the side of the tree and tore the door off its hinges. He reached in and grabbed Yesterday George and Yesterday Harold in his mighty, metallic hand.

"I'VE GOT YOU NOW!" roared the preposterous porcelain predator, as he shook the two boys back and forth. The three fuzzy creatures fell to the floor. Quickly, they got to their feet and excitedly flapped their wings. They weren't sure what was happening, but it seemed like fun.

The Turbo Toilet 2000 jumped down from the tree house and squeezed the two boys tightly in his fist.

"Finally, I shall avenge my fallen allies and take my place as the SUPREME LEADER OF THE EARTH!" he shouted.

The three tiny creatures fluttered down to Yesterday George and Yesterday Harold, wagging their little tails with excitement. But when they saw the looks of terror on the boys' faces, they realized that this was not a game.

Quickly, the three creatures took action and began circling the Turbo Toilet 2000 like mosquitoes. Then they each took turns zooming in close and taking quick bites out of him with their bionic jaws.

"OUCH!" cried the Turbo Toilet 2000, as he desperately swatted at the swooping creatures. "What the heck ARE those things?"

Another one dived in, bit him on the forearm and yanked out a steel bolt.

"HEY! CUT THAT OUT!" screamed the frustrated fiend, as he released the boys and began swatting at the flying beasties with all his might.

The strange furry creatures grasped the Turbo Toilet 2000 by his lid and shoulders and lifted him off the ground. Flapping their wings as hard as they could, they carried the villainous lavatory higher and higher into the air.

LEFT HAND HERE

IT'S MY POTTY
AND I'LL FLY
IF I WANT TO.

209

RIGHT
THUMB
HERE

IT'S MY POTTY
AND I'LL FLY
IF I WANT TO.

Soon they were almost a kilometre up in the sky.

"LEMME GO! LEMME GO!" roared the terrified Turbo Toilet 2000. This turned out to be a poor choice of words, because the three fuzzy creatures did exactly that.

All at once, they released their grip on the evil, robotic behemoth, and sent him tumbling downward. Faster and faster he fell through the clouds, spinning out of control and screaming in terror.

CHAPTER 33
TO MAKE A LONG STORY SHORT

CHAPTER 34

WELCOME BACK, KRUPP

The Turbo Toilet 2000 had smashed into a vacant parking lot and exploded with a sonic boom that shattered nearly every window in the city.

When the smoke finally cleared, Mr Krupp sat alone in the centre of the impact point, surrounded by mangled metal and jagged chunks of porcelain. Everything around him had been destroyed, but Mr Krupp, surprisingly, was unharmed. His super powers had protected him.

Soon, two cops arrived at the scene. "Are you OK?" they asked.

"I guess so," said Mr Krupp. "This must be one of those crazy nightmares I keep having!"

"Oh, *great*!" said Officer McWiggly. "It looks like we've got another naked schoolteacher who thinks he's *dreaming*!"

"Let's lock him up with the others," said the chief of police.

CHAPTER 35
HAMSTERDACTYLS

George and Harold finally made it home just as the three furry creatures were returning to the tree house. Yesterday George and Yesterday Harold told them what had happened, and how the strange, fuzzy creatures inside Crackers's eggs had saved the Earth from total destruction.

"What *are* these things anyway?" asked George.

"They kinda look like a cross between a hamster and a pterodactyl," said Harold.

"Eewww!" said George. "That means that Sulu and Crackers w-w-were— EEEWWWW!"

"But that doesn't make sense," said Harold. "How could a mammal mate with a reptile?"

"EEEEWWWWW!" cried George again.

"I mean, unless Sulu's DNA was mutated when he morphed with that bionic endoskeleton," said Harold.

"EEEEEWWWWWW!" cried George again.

"I suppose a mammal with mutated genes *MIGHT* be able to breed with a prehistoric reptile," Harold speculated.

"What part of *EEEEEEWWWWWWW* don't you understand?!!?" shouted George.

"Sorry," said Harold.

Soon, the four friends and their three new pets were back up in their tree house. They all worked together to clean up the mess. Then, the two Harolds made beds for the baby hamsterdactyls out of shoe boxes, while the two Georges thought up names for them.

"Let's call the girl *Dawn*," said George.

"What about the two boys?" asked Yesterday Harold.

"*Orlando* and *Tony*," said Yesterday George.

Harold wrote their new pets' names on their shoe box beds, but he still seemed perplexed.

"Are you *still* trying to figure out how we ended up with three half-pterodactyl, half-bionic-hamster pets?" asked George.

"Yeah, sort of," Harold replied.

"You're thinking too much," said George. "Listen, if you look too closely at these stories, they're gonna fall apart completely. Whaddya think this is, *Shakespeare*?!!?"

"I guess you're right," said Harold.

"Of course I'm right," said George. "Just go with it, man."

CHAPTER 36

ALL'S WELL THAT ENDS POORLY

"Well, that was a satisfying ending," said Yesterday Harold, as he tucked Tony, Orlando, and Dawn into their beds.

"What do you mean, *satisfying*?" said George. "The city is destroyed, our teachers are in jail, there are *four* of us and our three mutant pets think we're their *mums*!"

"Oh, yeah," said Yesterday Harold. "I guess there *are* a lot of loose ends in this story."

"Uh-oh," said Harold. "That can only mean one thing!"

"What?" asked Yesterday George.

Dawn   Orlando   Tony

"Another *SEQUEL*!!!" said Harold.

"OH, *NO!*" whined George and Yesterday George.

"Here we go again!!!" moaned Harold and Yesterday Harold.

ABOUT THE AUTHOR

When Dav Pilkey was a kid, he suffered from ADHD, dyslexia and behavioural problems. Dav was so disruptive in class that his teachers made him sit out in the hall every day. Fortunately, Dav loved to draw and make up stories. He spent his time in the hallway creating his own original comic books.

In the second grade, Dav Pilkey created a comic book about a superhero named Captain Underpants. His teacher ripped it up and told him he couldn't spend the rest of his life making silly books.

Fortunately, Dav was not a very good listener.